Text copyright © 1997 Rob Childs
Illustrations copyright © 1997 Gini Wade

The right of Rob Childs to be identified as the author of this
work and the right of Gini Wade to be identified as the illustrator
of this work has been asserted to them in accordance with the
Copyright, Designs and Patents Act 1988.

This edition first published in Great Britain in 1997 by
Macdonald Young Books, an imprint of Wayland Publishers Ltd

Typeset in 15/22 Veljovic Book by Roger Kohn Designs
Printed and bound in Belgium by Proost N. V.

Macdonald Young Books
61 Western Road
Hove
East Sussex BN3 1JD

British Library Cataloguing in Publications Data available

ISBN 0 7500 2114 4
ISBN 0 7500 2115 2 (pb)

Drake
AND THE
Devon Boy

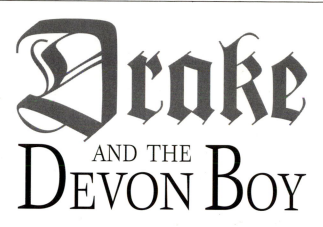

Rob Childs
Illustrated by Gini Wade

MACDONALD YOUNG BOOKS

1
Land Ahoy!

Nine year old Robin Newman was freezing cold, soaking wet and scared out of his wits.

Angry waves lashed into the cabin boy's face as they toppled across the heaving deck of the *Golden Hind.* He clung to the ropes around the bottom of a mast, choking on sea water.

With each roll of the ship, Robin struggled to keep his grip as the icy water swirled back over the sides. The force of it sucked at his legs, trying to drag him away into the depths. Somehow he hung on.

The black night was full of the most
terrifying sounds, as if the ship itself were
breaking up. Its masts bent and groaned
and the howling winds rattled the sail
rigging like ghostly chains.

6

Worst of all to Robin's ears were the desperate cries of the crew. Crouched nearby was Old Jack, the ship's cook, his eyes wide with fear. "Mercy!" he screamed and Robin saw him clutch a silver cross around his neck. "Lord have mercy upon us!"

"Too late for all that, Jack," shouted the master-gunner, Ned. "Put your faith in Francis Drake. The General is the only one who can save us now!"

He was wrong. Next morning, after weeks of storms, the winds suddenly dropped as if by a miracle. Everyone, including their captain, fell to their knees in thankful prayer.

Francis Drake's loud voice rang out over the deck. "Praise be to God that our lives have been spared."

"Aye," grumbled the cook, "but we won't live much longer unless we get some fresh food and water soon. What we have left is rotten and foul."

"Do you know where we are, General?" asked the master-gunner.

Drake cast around for any sign of land. There was none. The *Golden Hind* had entered uncharted waters. "Yes and no, Ned!" he laughed. "The gales have blown us clean through the Straits of Magellan and far beyond. I will study the compass and set our course to the north at last."

Their captain ran his hands over his thick, salt-matted hair. "Be brave and be proud, all of you," he cried. "We are the first Englishmen to sail the Pacific Ocean!"

Robin tried to be brave, too. He had a lot to live up to with the General being his uncle. Old Jack often pulled his leg about that.

"Here he comes," the cook cackled
if ever the little cabin boy crept into the
galley. "Who'd have thought the nephew of
Francis Drake, England's finest sea captain,
would keep sneakin' in here to pinch one
of me biscuits?"

Several days later, while Robin was helping Old Jack boil up the last of the salted, stinking, maggoty beef, the General summoned him on deck. "Boy, bring me my pens and charts."

Robin obeyed instantly. "Look, Boy, the frigate bird!" his uncle boomed, slapping him on the back. "And you know what that means..."

Robin spied the forked tail and long, slender wings as it skimmed over the ship to snatch a fish from another bird's beak in mid-flight. He remembered that the frigate bird was never seen on the water. It always returned to land to rest.

Soon there was a wild cry from the top of the main mast. "Land ahoy!" shrieked sharp-eyed Kit, clinging to his swaying perch. "Land ahoy!"

The crew rushed to view the distant
hills and began dancing round the deck in
their filthy rags. Even Old Jack joined in
the fun, pounding a large spoon on a metal
bucket in time to their steps.

Drake laughed heartily and started to
sketch an outline of the coast on his charts.
"Boy!" he commanded. "Fetch wine from
my cabin. This calls for celebration."

Robin ran to do his uncle's bidding as the General promised riches to his loyal crew. "We shall be like the pirate frigate bird," he told them. "We'll seize the treasures of the Spanish from out of their very mouths."

"Aye, they've had things their own way for too long in the Pacific," grinned Ned. "We'll soon show those greedy Spaniards that their gold isn't safe from our cannons here now, just like in the Atlantic."

"Let them fear the name of Francis Drake in both the mighty oceans of this world!" the General boasted and lifted up his golden goblet to give the toast. "We do all this, men, for the glory of God and for England, in the name of Her Majesty, Queen Elizabeth!"

Young Robin drained his own glass of wine in one great gulp. It made a nice change from the stale beer he and the crew were used to drinking!

2
Arise, Sir Francis!

"*El Draque!* It is the Dragon!"

Francis Drake smiled when he heard the Spanish settlers cry out his name. As soon as they saw the *Golden Hind* drop anchor in Salada Bay, they fled into the hills in terror.

"My reputation seems to have got here ahead of me," he laughed. "Come, let's refill our larders and water barrels from their stores."

While the carpenters and sail makers repaired the damage caused by the storms, the General rowed ashore with some of the crew. The port had been left undefended and they collected vital supplies to take back on board.

That evening Robin served his uncle a feast of spiced pork, fish and cheese, eaten off silver plates decorated with his own coat of arms.

"I'm told that the Spaniards think I'm a wizard!" the General joked as he wined and dined with Ned. "They even say I have a magic mirror in my cabin which lets me see their ships from far away."

"They sure won't see *us* coming," the master-gunner grinned. "They'll be in for a shock when we suddenly sail over the horizon towards them."

Robin kept dreaming about the magic mirror. He searched everywhere for it when he cleaned the cabin, but there was nothing to be found.

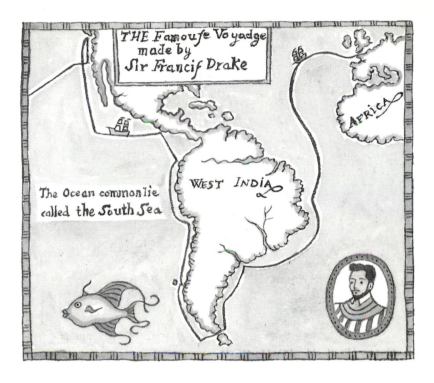

The map shows:

THE Famouse Voyadge made by Sir Francis Drake

AFRICA

The Ocean commonlie called the South Sea

WEST INDIA

Ned's forecast proved true. As the months went by, the *Golden Hind* raided Spanish harbours and treasure ships up the long Pacific coastline of the American continent. Robin was amazed at all the jewels, precious stones, silver and gold that were loaded into the hold. The extra weight made the small wooden ship settle lower and lower in the water.

"No need to look so worried, Boy, I'll make sure we don't sink," the General chuckled, slipping a gold coin into his nephew's hand.

Further north still, Drake went ashore again to explore. "I name this land New Albion," he announced, placing an English silver sixpence on the ground to stake his claim. "It now belongs to Queen Elizabeth."

"How do we get home from here?"
Robin asked timidly.

"We shall head westwards across the
ocean," Drake said, his blue eyes gleaming
at the thought. "God willing, Boy, we shall
sail right around the world back to England!"

"Do we have charts to show us the way?"

The General shook his head. "There
aren't any. We have to draw our own as we
go along!"

Ten weeks later, the *Golden Hind* reached the Spice Islands, but this time it wasn't Kit who sighted land. Poor Kit had died from scurvy on the voyage, a disease that claimed many other victims, too, among the crew.

They set off again with tonnes of expensive spices crammed into the hold. But the ship soon hit a rocky reef below the waves and stuck fast.

"Cast off the heavy cannons into the sea," the General told Ned, but still the *Golden Hind* did not move.

"We will have to throw part of the gold away," he sighed.

When that had no effect either, some of
the spices were also tossed overboard. The
water around the ship changed colour and
bubbled up as the pepper, nutmeg and
cloves began to dissolve.

"It's no good, General, we're well and truly trapped," Ned reported. "All the treasure in the world can't save us now."

"We're doomed!" cried Old Jack, starting to gabble his prayers.

"Quiet, old man!" the General commanded, hauling the cook off his knees. "See, the wind's changed direction. It's filling the sails again. With a bit of luck, we might just yet escape..."

They could hear the harsh sound of wood scraping against rock and everyone held their breath. Suddenly, the ship slid off the reef and floated free, undamaged, back into deeper water.

Robin was twelve years old when the *Golden Hind* eventually arrived in Plymouth, the town of his birth, one September day in 1580. The local people had last seen the ship, known then as the *Pelican,* three years before. They gave Francis Drake, a Devon man himself, a hero's welcome.

The following spring, the *Golden Hind,* festooned with coloured flags, sailed triumphantly up the River Thames to London on her final voyage. Robin had the honour of serving at a large oak table when Queen Elizabeth came to dine on deck with his uncle.

"I am well pleased with all the gifts that you brought back from your travels," Her Majesty smiled, listening to the General's personal four-piece orchestra. "Now hand me your sword and kneel down."

For once, the General was taken by surprise as Queen Elizabeth placed the sword lightly upon both of his shoulders. "Arise, *Sir* Francis Drake, my bold knight," she announced grandly. "The first Englishman to sail around the world!"

3
Eight Years Later

"Robin, take charge of loading the ship," Sir Francis said to his nephew. "I'm going to keep watch with the Lord High Admiral up on Plymouth Hoe."

It was Friday, the 19th of July, 1588, Robin Newman's twentieth birthday. Now one of his uncle's most trusted officers, Robin celebrated the day by preparing for battle – against the might of the Spanish Armada!

Robin leaned over the starboard side of the General's flagship, the *Revenge*. "Come on, make haste," he told the merchants on their carts below. "Get those barrels up here quickly. Then go and fetch more."

His voice was almost lost in all the noise. Men's shouts, whistles and laughter were mixed with the harsh screeches of gulls, eager to swoop down for any scraps of food.

The birds were not the only ones on the look-out. Long before the huge fleet of Spanish ships sighted Lizard Point in Cornwall, they had already been spotted. A series of beacon fires were lit to warn of the Armada's slow, steady advance up the English Channel.

Robin hurried to report the news to
his uncle himself. He found the new Vice-
Admiral of the Queen's Navy calmly playing
bowls on top of the cliffs of the Hoe.

Sir Francis paused, stroked his beard and winked at him. "Fear not, Robin," he chuckled loudly. "There's time yet to finish this game of bowls and then go and beat those Spanish!"

Sir Francis knew there was no need to rush. The south-west wind would make it difficult to get the ships out of Plymouth harbour until high tide. He also knew how his joking would help keep up the spirits of all the English sailors.

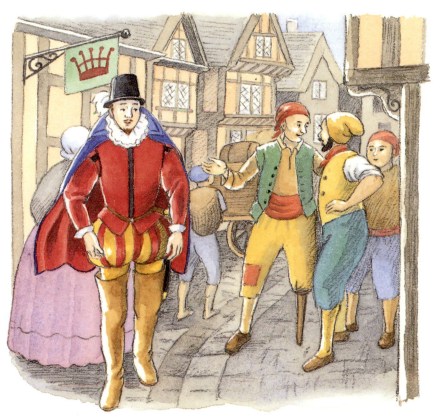

Robin enjoyed their excited gossip as
he walked back to the harbour along the
narrow, twisting streets of the Barbican.
"Heard what the General said?" cackled
one seaman with a toothless grin. "He's
afraid o' nothin'. There's no way we can
lose with captains like him."

Jostling through the crowds, Robin squeezed past swaying, overflowing carts to reach the *Revenge*. It was his job to beat the ship's large drum to summon the crew from the packed town. Drake's Drum, everyone called it.

Extra barrels of gunpowder, food and water were loaded aboard and the ships set out during the night. It wasn't until daylight that Robin gazed upon the splendour of the Armada in full sail. Over 130 vessels swept by in half-moon formation, their great galleons seeming as tall as castles.

"Aye, we may be outnumbered, Robin," Sir Francis said grimly, "but with God on our side, our swift, gallant ships will not be outfought!"

Fierce clashes took place all along
the south coast over the next few days,
preventing the Armada from landing on
English soil. The *Revenge* was always in the
thick of the action, the General's face and
white silk shirt streaked with sweat and
dirt as he worked on deck with his crew.

He rescued a squadron of ships under attack off Portland Bill, captured a damaged galleon, the *Rosario*, and crippled another with accurate cannon-fire. Finally, however, the Armada managed to find shelter near the French port of Calais, hoping to pick up thousands more Spanish troops from the mainland of Europe to support the invasion of England.

Sir Francis took Robin to an urgent
meeting on board the Lord High Admiral's
Ark Royal, to discuss possible tactics.
"Let's use fireships!" the General advised
forcefully. "Put the fear of the devil into
them!"

"Good idea," agreed Lord Howard. "I
shall have some old boats sent to us from
Dover."

"We can't afford to wait," Robin heard his
uncle argue. "We must sacrifice some of our
ships here and strike before it is too late."

Sir Francis had his own way, as usual, and Robin helped prepare the 200 tonne *Thomas*. It was filled with bundles of twigs, covered with tar and hauled up beside seven others. He also volunteered to steer the *Thomas* towards the Armada, escaping by rowing boat after igniting the fuses.

At midnight on the last Sunday in July, the sky was ablaze as the burning devil-ships drifted on the tide. The vivid red light reflected eerily on the water.

As the Spanish fleet cut their anchor cables and scuttled out to sea to flee the flames, Robin saw sailors jumping for their

lives into the frothing waves. One of the Spanish flagships, the *San Lorenzo*, even ran aground on the shore.

"There's a storm brewing up!" exclaimed Robin. "They won't be able to retreat along the Channel now. We've got them on the run!"

All through the following day, the disorganised Armada suffered a terrible pounding, losing several galleons. Not a single English ship was sunk in the battle, but both sides were almost out of ammunition.

"That's enough, we'll let nature do the rest," the General decided. "Mark my words, the gales will wreck a lot more of their ships as they try and get round our rocky northern coasts back to Spain."

By the time the *Revenge* arrived home
in Plymouth, tales were already being told
in the Barbican taverns about the great
victory. Robin had a few to tell himself, but
he let others boast about his uncle's deeds.

"Whenever England's in danger," one old sailor cried out, waving his tankard of ale in the air, "I reckon Drake's Drum will beat all on its own, if need be, to call Sir Francis to come and save us again!"